One More
Makes Four

One More Makes Four

pictures by Almut Gernhardt
with verses by Robert Gernhardt

translated from the German by
Elizabeth Watson Taylor

Jonathan Cape · Thirty Bedford Square · London

The day begins with light and noise,
and steam-boat hoots; but see!
Three cats upon the river-bank
are sitting silently.

The sun is hot: time to go home;
the roast is done for eating.
These cats sit on immovably,
pricking their ears and waiting.

The sun goes down, and night draws near.
An owl hoots in the copse.
The three cats sit, just as before,
and lick their little chops.

Now it is dark, and all is still.
The half-moon shines on high.
The first cat speaks in earnest tones:
"We have been told a lie.

"The Water-Mouse does not exist.
The fox was only joking,
and we have waited here for hours!
It really is provoking."

The other cats are most upset;
their empty stomachs rumble.
Three cats upon the river-bank
feel both ashamed and humble.

Walking in the street by day,
you are not alone.
Your shadow follows silently
over stick and stone.
This we know. But no one knows
where at night the shadow goes.

After nightfall – so they say –
shadows take a holiday,
and they meet in secret places,
shadows of all shapes and races,
and of Man and Beast and Bird
which, by day, don't say a word.
In the darkness they converse
till the light of day appears,
then they have to rush away.
Well, that is what people say;
in addition, they aver
(I don't know how right they are)
that some mischief-making loners
will not go back to their owners.
Shadows such as these, I'm told,
can one everywhere behold,
making trouble, that is sure,
when their masters they ignore.
Yes, they even walk behind
masters of a different kind!
Well, it might indeed be true,
so I'll tell you what to do:

Walking in the street by day
if you're not alone,
look behind and just make sure
that shadow is your own!

The fields are wrapped in darkness now;
the cat converses with the cow:

Cat: "One should not praise the day above the night."
Cow: "Well spoken from up there. You are quite right."

Cat: "Today I had quite an adventure!"
Cow: "Do tell me, for I'd love to hear!"

Cat: "It was with a dog that I came upon."
Cow: "Well, that could happen to anyone."

Cat: "Yes, but this one was seven yards high!"
Cow: "Seven yards? My goodness! You don't say!"

Cat: "Yes, and it could breathe out fire, too!"
Cow: "Good gracious! Is that really true?"

Cat: "Yes, and it ran right up to me!"
Cow: "Heavens! And did you turn and flee?"

Cat: "No. I just put my back up – so – "
Cow: "Ah – and you told him where to go?"

Cat: "Yes! I only said 'Miaow' – just once – not loud."
Cow: "And he ran off as fast as he could?"

Cat: "Exactly! Or I wouldn't be here."
Cow: "True enough. I like to have you near."

Cat: "And I you. You know how I feel all right."
Cow: "I'm glad that you are where you are. Goodnight!"

If the whole world treats you badly,
your friends as well as strangers –
there are those who'll help you gladly:
call the White Avengers.

Once the champions hear your call
nothing stays their speed.
Neither mountain, river, wall
nor hurricane they heed.

Straightway they stand before your door
just to make this plain:
"Tell those others WE are here,
if they bother you again!"

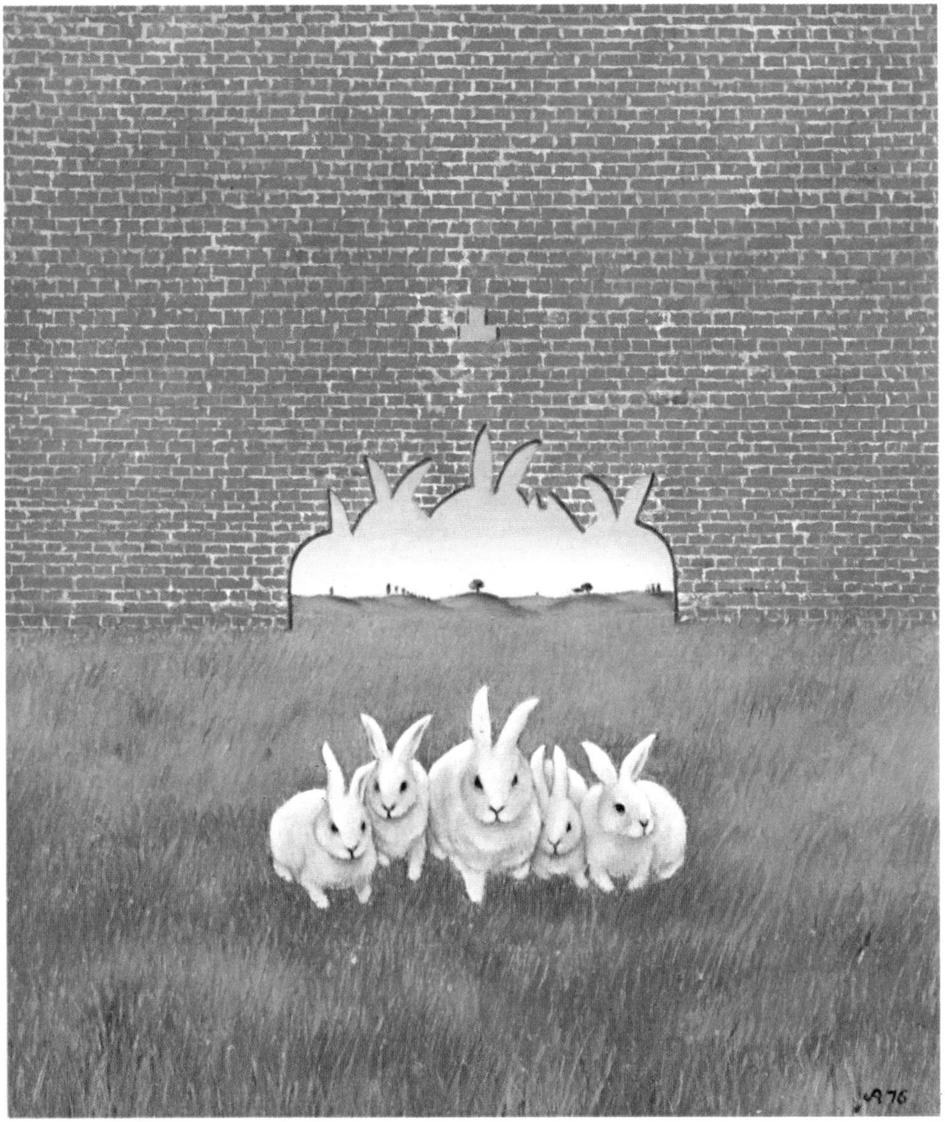

The room is light,
the bed is bare,
and yet I feel
there's someone there.

Is he dangerous?
Is he nice?
Is he a guest?
Or a thief in disguise?
Does he like me?
Or wish me dead?
Could he be hiding
under my bed?

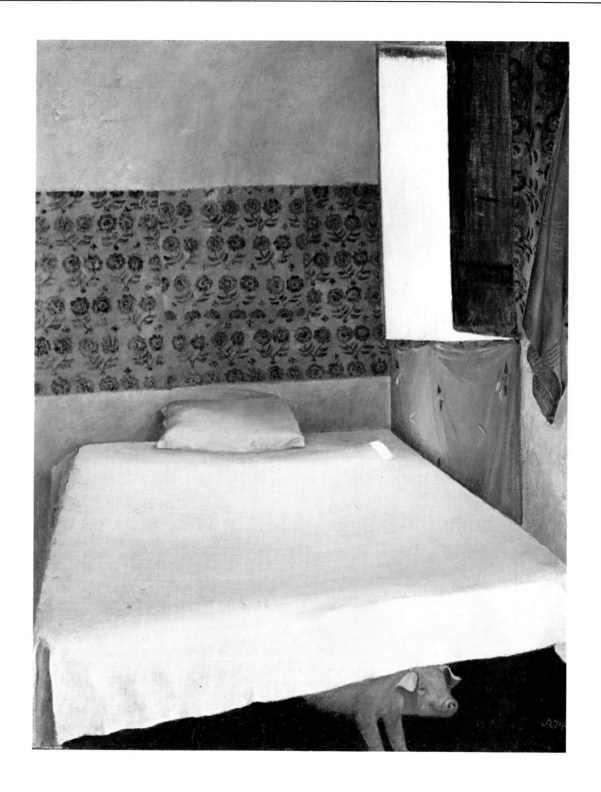

If I decide that in the garden
I will take my bowl of broth,
the black cat speaks to me, and says:
"You've got no table-cloth!"

After I have put the cloth on,
and am sitting in my chair,
the black cat miowls in a shrill voice:
"You haven't any table-ware!"

So I go and fetch a plate,
I feel so hungry I could swoon.
The black cat loudly screams at me:
"Why don't you bring a spoon?"

When I come back with a spoon
my soup at last to take,
I find the black cat sitting in it
and she begins to shriek:

"Just now when you were in the house,
a great big dog came by:
he drank the broth in one huge gulp,
and then he ran away!"

I eye the cat in disbelief;
my heart-beats can be heard.
Do I not see a drop of broth
suspended from her beard?

To climb upon a rainbow is the simplest thing to do
provided that you stick to these three well-tried rules and true:

First there must be rain, you know,
if there is to be a bow.
Secondly you have to try
pretty hard to climb so high.
Thirdly you should memorise
that which never must arise:
think of cowboys when you climb,
think of violins and wine,
think of palm-trees, think of beer,
blackbirds, thrushes, fish and steer.
Think of pearls and rubies rare
think of silver, think of gold,
but *never* think of either ear
otherwise you'll lose your hold.
At the faintest memory
of your ears you'd start to sway.
The sharpest claws could not prevent
your unavoidable descent.
All clear? Enjoy yourself a lot!
But *do not think of you-know-what!*

The worried hedgehog anxiously
gazes at distant hills and sky:

at hills, and at the distant view
where once he found his loved one true.

Ten hours ago, she disappeared,
without a wave, without a word.

"Where are you, dearest?" loud he cried.
"You pointed-snouted, lovely bride?

"You whose bristling prickle-beauty
drove me from the paths of duty?

"You whose dainty pawlets were
utterly beyond compare?

"You who squeaked so winningly
at every little kiss from me?

"Oh, do not leave me, dearest dear!
Or . . . what's that scraping sound I hear?

"That so familiar snorting noise
must surely be my loved one's voice!

"My darling, are you not quite near?"
"Yes, dearest," comes the answer clear:

"I must have had a nap or two:
I hope you can forgive me though."

And gently wafts the evening air
around the happy bridal pair.

The silent cat
on the table lying
is thinking about
a kippered herring.

Three cherries scattered
where she lies
are still and silent
as she is.

The kipper on
the shelf next door
finds all this silence
hard to bear.

He would gladly cry:
"Do make some remark!"
But because he is wise
he does not talk.

For if he did
he would be discovered.
So no one knows
he is in the cupboard.

Cat, cherries and kipper
do not speak
but the table gives
an occasional crrrrreak.

Pack your bag, and sail away
to those northern isles
where, upon a lonely quay,
a lion sits and smiles.

Shield in paws, and naught around
but sea-gulls and the sea.
He's been sitting there for years:
say "Hello" to him from me.

We have to move tomorrow, so we are
in a very awkward situation,
for we have to find a house at once
with the following accommodation:
eight rooms to meet in,
eight kitchens to eat in,
eight bathrooms to splash in,
eight passages to dash in,
eight stoves to keep us warm,
eight stairs to clamber on,
eight windows to sit in,
eight corners to spit in,
eight doors to be clawed at,
eight walls to be gnawed at,
a giant park all around,
price envisaged: one pound.

Do help us find another home.
We do so want to settle down.

The Meercat Family

At four a.m. before the dawn of day
the friendly kitchen-owl was heard to say:

"Which of you knows my favourite dish?
I'll bet you don't know what it is.
I'm sorry to hear that you have no idea –
but then, I didn't think you'd know:
so I'll give you three guesses, starting now!

"No, no! Who said it could be potatoes?
My favourite dish is as round as a ball,
I eat it with pepper and olive oil
and vinegar – but I'm giving away
too much, and this will spoil the show,
so guess again: there are two to go.

"Nonsense! It couldn't be avocados!
They are rough and green and shaped like a pear
while my favourite dish – you can see it here –
is smooth and red. So what IS its name?
Do try and think. There is still time
for you to have one final guess –
                and YES!" They are

Tomatoes!

Stop and listen, everyone!
Bertram Beaver's on the run!
Having vanished from his cage
he's in town on the rampage,
stealing edibles, and stuffing
anything that's in the offing.
Twenty pounds of streaky bacon
are among the things he's taken,
and we seek a vat of jam,
ten oranges, a leg of lamb,
fifty thousand chocolate-bars,
ninety eggs, and now, alas!
We are told that we must list
even more things that are missed:
biscuits, marzipan and toffee,
mixed fruit trifle, tea and coffee,
ices, puddings large and small,
Bertram will consume them all.
Therefore do not venture out
just in case he is about.

We will give a big reward
if you catch him:

                              Scotland Yard

Day and night three guardians sit
at this hedge – and won't permit
anyone to pass beyond them
who can't answer this conundrum:

It has a cover,
but isn't a pot.
It has a back,
but a head it has not.
It has many leaves,
but none are round.
It stands without feet,
it speaks without sound.
Who can't find the answer
may not enter our land.
So hurry and guess it.
You've got it in hand!

A book!

First published in Great Britain 1978
© Insel Verlag Frankfurt am Main 1976
Translation © 1978 by Jonathan Cape Ltd

ISBN 0 224 01577 X

Jonathan Cape Ltd, 30 Bedford Square, London WC1
Printed in Italy